THE SHADE
OF DEATH

KOLDO
THE ARCTIC-
WARRIOR

With special thanks to Michael Ford

To Charlie Heaphy

www.beastquest.co.uk

ORCHARD BOOKS
338 Euston Road, London NW1 3BH
Orchard Books Australia
Level 17/207 Kent St, Sydney, NSW 2000

A Paperback Original
First published in Great Britain in 2009

Beast Quest is a registered trademark of Working Partners Limited
Series created by Working Partners Limited, London

Text © Working Partners Limited 2009
Cover and inside illustrations by Steve Sims © Orchard Books 2009

A CIP catalogue record for this book is available from
the British Library.

ISBN 978 1 40830 440 2

7 9 10 8 6

Printed in the UK by CPI Bookmarque, Croydon, CR0 4TD

The paper and board used in this paperback are natural recyclable
products made from wood grown in sustainable forests. The
manufacturing processes conform to the environmental regulations of
the country of origin.

Orchard Books is a division of Hachette Children's Books,
an Hachette UK company

www.hachette.co.uk

KOLDO
THE ARCTIC-
WARRIOR

BY ADAM BLADE

ORCHARD BOOKS

THE ICE CASTLE

CRESCENT CAVE

FREESHOR

GWILDORIAN PLAINS

THE RAINBOW JUNGL

*W*elcome to a new world...

Did you think you'd seen all the evil that existed? You're almost as foolish as Tom! He may have conquered Wizard Malvel, but fresh challenges await him. He must travel far and leave behind everything he knows and loves. Why? Because he has six Beasts to defeat in a kingdom he can't even call home.

Will his heart be in it? Or will Tom turn his back on this latest Quest? Little does he know, but he has close ties to the people here. And a new enemy determined to ruin him. Can you guess who that enemy is...?

Read on to see how your hero fares.

Velmal

PROLOGUE

Linus gasped when he saw the giant footprint in the snowdrifts. The stories were true.

"It's this way!" said Dylar, pointing a bony finger along the icy path ahead.

Flames licked the air from the torch in his other hand, and grey smoke curled up into the freezing night sky. Dylar was the village elder, and the orange light showed every wrinkle on his stern face.

Linus was only a child, but he carried a torch like everyone else. Despite the heat from the flames, he shivered inside his thick fur clothes. His village, Freeshor, was covered in snow all year round, but tonight the cold got into his bones like never before.

They were hunting a monster.

"There! There!" shouted someone. "I saw something!"

Shouts went up among the people of the village.

"Where?"

"After the Beast!"

"There's no time to waste."

The crowd surged forward, but Dylar shouted louder than the rest: "Stop! Stay close together. We can't tackle this creature unless we work as a team. Send the young ones out of harm's way."

Linus made sure he wasn't among the children pushed to the rear. He slipped under hands and legs to stay near the front.

There's no way I'm going to miss the fun! he thought.

As the path dipped and narrowed, something glinted ahead.

"It's the ice man!" a man cried. Linus held his breath.

The creature was facing away from them, thickset and as tall as two men. Its frozen body shone pale blue in the reflected torchlight. In some places, Linus could see right through its torso.

The Beast turned to them, and bellowed in anger. His face was made of flat surfaces and angles, like a half-finished statue. Icicles hung from his chin and brows, and his eyes were like frozen pools. Linus saw that the Beast was carrying a shield, taller than Linus himself. It glowed a sickly green. In his other fist he clutched a jagged ice-club.

"Wh…what should we do?"
someone asked.

With a creaking sound, the Ice
Monster raised one foot, then
brought it down hard on the ground.
The path shook, and the villagers
stumbled backwards. But the creature
didn't come towards them.

"Surround him!" Dylar cried.

The front line surged forwards, and
Linus followed. The Ice Beast turned
to run, but the men of Freeshor were
quicker. The crowd split into two
columns that threaded either side of
the Beast. One villager leapt right
at the Beast's back, but he slipped
off into the snow. The Ice Giant
bellowed and lifted a foot to crush
him. Linus jumped forwards
brandishing his torch. The flames
jerked and flared before the Beast's

face and he backed away, dropping his shield and lifting one arm to protect himself.

Linus stared open-mouthed.

The Ice Beast was afraid of fire!

Small droplets of water were appearing all over the Beast's body as it stumbled among the circle of villagers, not daring to come close to the ring of blazing torches.

Linus inched forwards. If he could claim the shield, he'd be the talk of the village. Holding his torch out like a sword, he walked towards his prize. The Beast reached out for his shield with its thick, icy fingers, but Linus pushed his torch closer.

"Keep back!" he heard himself shout. The Beast withdrew. Linus tugged the heavy shield away and the men of Freeshor cheered.

The Beast looked more panicked than ever. Water poured off it in rivulets and it seemed to shrink.

"Destroy him!" shouted one of the villagers.

"Melt him!" shouted another.

The ring of fire began to close.

But Linus heard Dylar call out over the tumult.

"No!" The elder's face creased in a smile as everyone waited to hear what he would say. "There's another way…"

CHAPTER ONE

THE FIRST CHALLENGE

Tom could barely stay upright in his saddle as Storm picked his way down the mountain path. The Quests in Gwildor were tougher than anything he'd faced before and the battle with the last Beast, Rokk, had drained him of strength.

His hand throbbed with pain. Ever

since Krabb had injured him with his giant pincers, poison had been spreading through Tom's hand. Now he gripped the reins with his left hand and cradled the injured right one against his side. He looked around at Elenna, hoping she wouldn't notice.

I don't want her to worry, thought Tom. They were still only halfway through their Gwildorian mission, and there were three more Beasts to free from Velmal.

Suddenly, a shower of stones scattered from beneath Silver's feet, making him yelp. Crying out, Elenna slipped down from the saddle. Her pet was licking his paw, and Tom saw blood on the path.

"Is he all right?" Tom asked.

Elenna wrapped her arms around

Silver's neck.

"I think so," she said. Gently, she lifted the wolf's foot and inspected his paw. "It doesn't look like more than a scratch."

By the time Elenna remounted, Silver was back on his feet, anxious to get going. Elenna peered ahead down the rocky path.

"Maybe we should look at the amulet's map?" she said.

Tom took the silver amulet from around his neck and held it out in front of him. A piece of blue enamel sparkled in its centre. The amulet was formed of the six pieces he'd gathered from his Quests in the Forbidden Land. A map on the back of the amulet was guiding Tom through Gwildor.

Tom turned the amulet over. Two

roads branched across the north of Gwildor, where the land was white with snow and frozen lakes. One road led to the shape of a man. Tom peered closely and saw that the man's limbs were made not of flesh and bone, but ice. A name appeared in spidery script: *Koldo*.

The other road led to a nearby destination, and a tiny picture of a set of scales. That's where they would head first. In each of his Quests, the amulet had led him to a magical item that helped with the mission.

"What use is a set of scales?" asked Elenna, looking over his shoulder.

"Who knows?" Tom replied. "But I trust the amulet."

They rode along the track through the Gwildorian landscape. Like everything in Gwildor, the colours seemed too brilliant to believe: luscious grasses greener than any in Avantia, plants of every colour in the rainbow. It was hard to believe Gwildor was suffering under the wicked spells of the evil Wizard Velmal.

They reached the edge of a forest. Tom could barely see beyond the first few trees. The trunks and dense tangles of vines grew close together. Shreds of mist coiled around the treetops. No sounds came from inside the forest. There were no chattering bird calls or howling monkeys. Not even the rustle of leaves was to be heard. The air seemed stagnant and deadly.

"Maybe we should go around the forest," said Elenna.

Tom checked the map, and shook

his head. "The forest's too big," he said. "We don't have time."

Tom had another reason for wanting to go through the forest: it would give him a chance to practise using his sword. Now that his right hand was in so much pain, he'd need to use his left hand for any sword fighting.

He hacked through the vines and branches that blocked their path, experimenting with the different thrusts and slashes that seemed so easy with his right hand. Everything felt unnatural and clumsy, and it wasn't long before his shoulder burned with the effort. He was breathing hard.

"Are you all right?" asked Elenna.

Tom chopped down a tough fern, and winced. He could see daylight

ahead. "We're almost there."

Elenna put a hand on his forearm.

"Tom," she said, "you don't have to pretend everything is all right. I can see you're in pain. Why not let me take over for a while?"

Tom lowered his head, feeling shame burn his cheeks.

"I can't give in," he said. "If I can't cut down a few vines, how can we ever face Koldo?"

"Just as long as you know I'm here to help," said Elenna.

Tom thanked his friend, and decided to swap hands. He gripped the sword hilt with his right hand. The muscles felt stiff.

By the time they reached the edge of the forest, Tom was dripping with sweat. A cold wind whipped Tom's breath away. Spread out before them were the Icy Plains, gleaming pale

blue and white as far as Tom could see. Areas of grass were scattered like small islands amidst the snow, and stacks of ice rose in towers above the ground, whittled into craggy shapes by the freezing gales. There was no horizon. The land seemed to blend into the sky.

"It's beautiful!" Elenna exclaimed.

Beautiful, Tom thought, *and deadly, too*.

CHAPTER TWO

INTO THE DARKNESS

Storm's hooves were soon clearing
a path through the patches of snow.

"It's like a different world!" said
Elenna. Her breath formed white
clouds in the air. "And so cold!"

Tom halted Storm while they put
on the furs that they kept in his
saddlebag. Silver, with his thick coat,
didn't seem to notice the cold and

jumped in the snowdrifts excitedly.

They trotted onwards, and soon the path disappeared. They were crossing a desert of snow. Flurries of icy flakes blew across their path, and one side of Tom's face was already numb.

"I don't know how long we can last out here," he said.

Mountain glaciers rose up around them, and Tom steered Storm into their shadow, out of the driving winds. The snow was like nothing Tom had ever seen in Avantia. The snowflakes glittered like crystals, and he had to squint against the reflected gleam of the sun. Silver padded on through the drifts, stopping often to shake the loose snow from his thick coat.

Tom consulted the amulet every hundred paces or so. *If we get lost here,* he thought, *we might never find our way out again. And Koldo will never be freed.*

Tom checked the amulet again and saw that they were closing in on the scales, located in a large, crescent-shaped cave. The map showed two entrances, one at each end.

Hopefully, that meant they could go straight through without having to double-back. Without the scales, Tom couldn't face Koldo. Liberating the Beast would be another step closer to helping Freya escape from Velmal.

If she can be freed, he thought to himself grimly.

The first entrance to the cave appeared in the side of a glacier ahead. It stood out sharply; a black hole in the vast expanse of whiteness. Tom and Elenna jumped down from Storm's back.

"The second entrance must be hidden on the other side of the glacier," said Elenna.

"The animals can't come with us," Tom said, as clouds of his breath froze in the air. "Storm will find it difficult to climb that slope of ice. We need to get in and out of the cave quickly." He could see that the tips of Elenna's hair were covered in frost. "But it's too cold to leave them out here."

"I know what to do," said Elenna, her eyes lighting up. She unlooped Storm's reins and tied them loosely around Silver's chest and front legs, like a harness. She gave a sharp whistle and Silver began to walk in a large circle with Storm following.

"That should keep them warm," said Elenna.

Tom smiled at his friend's cleverness. "Let's go," he said. "We still need to be quick."

They scrambled up the slope to the cave entrance, slipping and holding onto each other for support. Tom struggled to find a grip with his injured hand, and Elenna helped him up to the mouth of the cave. Peering

into the dark interior, the air seemed
even colder. There was a curious
animal smell too. It took Tom's eyes a
few moments to adjust to the gloom,
but then he felt a prickle of fear. The
entrance was narrow, and lined with
jagged rocks.

"Look," Elenna whispered, pointing
to the ground. Some small feathers
were floating in a shallow puddle.
Tom put his finger to his lips to let
Elenna know they needed to keep
quiet. If something did live here, it
wouldn't be used to visitors – he was
sure of that.

They stepped into the darkness of
the cave and felt their way along.
The only sound was their breathing
and the *drip, drip, drip* of water. Tom
had rearranged his scabbard so that
his sword hilt was in easy reach of

his uninjured left hand, but already his fingers were turning numb with cold. Elenna's teeth were chattering and he knew it wouldn't be long before his own would be doing the same.

Tom held out his shield on his right arm. The bell that Nanook the snow monster had given him long ago would help to protect them against some of the cold in the cave. He rubbed the bell gently and felt the space around them become warm, as though they were stepping through a current of hot air.

"Thank you," Elenna whispered.

Tom's eyes gradually adjusted as they shuffled along a passage. It widened into a cavernous space. Tom checked the amulet. According to the map, they were almost on top of the scales.

A rustling sound came from ahead.

Tom used his left hand to pull the sword out of his scabbard – and almost dropped it straight away. The weight of the blade felt unfamiliar.

Come on! he urged himself. *Concentrate!*

He tightened his grip on the hilt.

Shadows climbed the walls – terrible, crawling shapes. Suddenly the air was filled with violent squawking.

"Get down!" Tom cried.

He and Elenna dropped to their knees, as something flapped around them, screeching.

When the sound had passed, Tom climbed hesitantly to his feet.

"What was that?" asked Elenna, turning back.

The noise came again, and this time Tom stayed standing. Five squat birds

strode from around the corner.
Beady eyes glittered menacingly.
They each had a shiny black body,
and a fat white belly. Their beaks
were bright yellow and their short
wings didn't look very good for
flying. Every so often one launched
off the ground and fluttered a few
paces, before flopping down onto its
webbed feet.

"Don't they look silly!" Elenna
laughed.

Tom lowered his sword. As the
birds got closer he saw that their
feathers were matted and slimy. The
stench of rot filled his nostrils. The
birds darted around Tom and Elenna,
pecking at their calves, seeming to
challenge them to a fight. Despite
their greasy feathers, the birds' eyes
glowed with light – an evil light.

"I think these are Velmal's creatures," Tom said.

At the mention of the evil wizard's name, the birds began squawking. One leapt up and landed on Tom's shield, grasping it with gnarled claws. While Tom was shaking it loose, another jumped and stabbed its beak at his face. Tom shook them off, and Elenna kicked out with her feet. Tom swung his sword in front of the birds, as a warning.

I don't want to hurt them, he thought. *But they won't get the better of me.*

The creatures turned and flapped away towards the mouth of the cave and, as they vanished, their screeching seemed to turn to cackling laughter.

"Come on," Tom said, racing across the slippery floor of the cave. "Look!"

"The scales," Elenna gasped. There they were at the far side of the cave, shining out from their resting place in an alcove in the cave wall. Their brass glinted in the weak light that streamed down from cracks in the cave roof.

"We have to get Freya's prize!" Tom cried.

CHAPTER THREE

AN ENEMY AWAKES

Tom heard Elenna behind him, then a hand gripped his shoulder.

"Tom!" she whispered. "Look at the walls."

Tom glanced where Elenna was pointing. Now that they were closer, he could see that the scales were trapped in a sheet of ice.

"Well, the Quest is never simple, is it?" he said, grinning.

Together they walked over. Tom ran his hand over the surface of the ice, which must have been as thick as his arm. Close up, the scales shimmered like gold. Tom could see that they were delicate, not like the ones the market traders used in his village. What use could they be on a Beast Quest?

"How can we get them out?" asked Elenna.

"Perhaps I can use my sword to chip away—" Tom began to say.

Elenna clapped her hand over his mouth. Her eyes were wide with fright as she nodded at something over his shoulder. Tom turned.

Not ten paces away lay a white bear bigger than any Tom had ever seen. It was stretched out, eyes closed, with its head resting on its front legs. The animal's claws, yellow and gnarled, were as long as Tom's fingers but looked as sharp as eagle's talons. Bones and skulls of long-dead creatures were scattered around it.

Prickles of sweat broke out across Tom's skin.

Elenna motioned with her head, jerking it in the direction they'd come. Her meaning was clear: *Shall we go back?*

Tom turned towards the sleeping creature. If it woke up, the bear would be angry. Tom couldn't risk either of them being injured... But they couldn't go back. How could they hope to free Koldo whilst the magical scales were still trapped behind the ice?

Tom put his mouth to Elenna's ear. "We've got to get the scales," he whispered.

Elenna's jaw clenched with determination. "Then do it quietly!" she replied.

Tom drew his sword, and as the blade slipped from the scabbard, the metal let out a hiss against the leather. The bear shifted slightly and twitched its black nose.

Elenna drew an arrow and placed the shaft against her bow. Tom knew she wouldn't kill a defenceless animal, but if the bear woke and saw a weapon trained on it, it might think twice about attacking.

Tom placed the tip of his sword against the ice, using his good hand to steady the blade. He leaned into the hilt with his shoulder. A flake sheared away and clattered onto the ground. Tom felt a bead of sweat fall from his brow and watched it splash against the cave floor, immediately freezing to the ground.

I have to do this, he thought. *Come on!* He pressed again until another sliver of ice fell away. This was going to be long, slow work.

What about…? An idea formed in Tom's head.

He put his sword aside, and Elenna gave him a puzzled look. Tom lifted his shield to the wall. If Nanook's bell could keep them warm, maybe it could warm the ice, too. Elenna understood and smiled.

In a short time, the surface of the ice broke into beads of water. Drips began to fall. Slowly, in a wave of pulsing heat, the ice thinned. Alert, Tom watched the sleeping bear. The animal's flanks heaved with huge breaths.

Suddenly the ice gave a groan and a great section began to slip away. With a crash, the chunk of ice hit the ground and shattered.

Elenna and Tom stared at the

bear, frozen to the spot.

"Not now," Tom muttered. "Not when we're so close."

He willed the bear to carry on sleeping, but with a groan of despair, Tom saw the bear's jaws open in a mighty yawn. He caught a glimpse of its long white teeth against the red of its throat.

They'd woken the bear.

The animal shifted lazily, stretching its legs, then it raised its head and spotted Tom and Elenna. Its lips peeled back in a growl as it leapt up, standing on its two hind legs. Now, Tom could see just how massive it was; it was at least twice his own height and would have even dwarfed Storm.

The bear roared. Tom and Elenna were blasted with hot, stinking breath. Strings of spittle stretched between its jaws. Tom could not tear his eyes away from the bear's hooked claws.

The bear dropped down to its front legs again and began to run – straight towards them. Tom saw Elenna's bow dangling uselessly from her hand. She stared in terror as the bear galloped across the cave floor, its body heaving from side to side. It would be on them in moments.

"What do we do?" Elenna managed to ask.

Tom knew he had to think of something fast – before the bear ended the Quest, and their lives, for good.

CHAPTER FOUR

A NARROW ESCAPE

The bear let out a mighty roar and leapt forwards. Elenna dragged Tom out of the way, only just in time.

Their attacker crashed into the wall of ice, sending shards flying through the air like daggers. The bear cried out in pain as his nose collided against the cave wall. He reared up and let out another stench-filled roar, turning to face Tom and Elenna. Now the massive creature stood between them and the scales.

"Thanks for saving me! Now stay back," Tom warned Elenna. She nodded, backing reluctantly away.

The bear lumbered towards him, and swiped out with a paw. Tom ducked beneath the scything claws and looked for a way to get to the scales. But the bear was too big. When it came at him again, Tom swung his sword. The bear roared and shuffled back, snapping its drooling jaws. Strings of saliva fell onto the cave floor. It padded forwards, the ground reverberating with each step, forcing Tom to back away. He swung his sword through the air, but the blade didn't stop the animal's relentless approach. Slowly, Tom was being pushed backwards.

"I have an idea," Elenna cried.
"Throw me the amulet." Trusting his
companion, Tom tossed it to her.
"Can you hold him back?" she asked.

There was a sudden movement
beside Tom's face and he brought his
shield up into the air, just in time to
block a blow from the bear's mighty
fist. The force of the strike
reverberated along his injured hand,
and he swallowed back his pain.

"I think so," he grimaced. "But
hurry."

And Elena was gone, backing
towards the mouth of the cave.

Tom was alone. He advanced
towards the bear, cutting arcs through
the air with his blade. Pain made him
cry out and the bear's eyes seemed to
narrow with pleasure. Tom passed the
sword into his left hand.

He wouldn't be able to fight very well, but what choice did he have? As he thrust the sword towards the bear, the hilt caught on a jagged piece of rock. Without the strength in his hand to hold it firmly, the sword clattered to the ground.

It landed at the bear's feet and Tom darted forwards to grab it. A paw swung down and, although Tom threw himself to one side, he was too slow. The bear hit Tom, smashing him against the cold cave wall. The bear lumbered towards him, jaws wide. Tom got unsteadily to his feet, blood trickling down his cheek.

Something flashed behind the bear, and Tom's heart leapt. Elenna! How had she got there? Then he remembered: the second entrance! He could see his friend's head and shoulders on the other side of a tiny opening, peering into the cave.

Beyond her, Tom could see Storm's legs. Elenna put her fingers in her mouth and let out a shrill whistle.

The bear turned clumsily to look at her. But not for long. He turned back towards Tom, and growled fiercely.

"Elenna, distract him again!" Tom cried out.

She whistled again, but this time the bear ignored her, lunging at Tom, its paws scything the air. Tom stumbled backwards. There was a sudden hiss through the air and then – *thwock!*

The bear bellowed, spinning around. Tom saw one of Elenna's arrows sticking into its foot. It wasn't enough to seriously injure such a huge animal, but it was guaranteed to get its attention.

"It's now or never!" Tom muttered to himself.

Tom flung his sword through the air. It sailed towards the cave wall above the bear's head, and the point lodged into the ice. The bear turned on him again, but Tom was ready. He ran forwards, gaining speed all the time.

The bear lunged for him but Tom placed a foot against the cave wall, kicking off to leap into the air, reaching for the sword's hilt. The fingers of his left hand grabbed it.

Tom swung his legs over the bear's head, keeping hold of the sword. It came loose and Tom dropped onto the cave floor behind the bear. He was now beside the scales, and he snatched them from their resting place.

Tom scrambled towards the second entrance.

"Stay back!" Elenna called. "We need to make this bigger."

"OK. But hurry!" Tom called, crouching down and looking nervously over his shoulder. Thank goodness for the bear's size. It had followed him but its huge body was struggling to squeeze into the low space at the second entrance. But for how long?

Tom covered his head as ice showered over him. Storm was using his hooves to kick at the sides of the second entrance. Soon, there was just enough room for Tom to slide out of the cave into the snow.

"Thank you," he gasped, as he brushed the flakes away. The bear's roar filled the cave behind him, and its angry face, dribbling saliva, peeked out of the narrow opening.

But Tom was safe. It would be impossible for the bear to squeeze through. He stood up and patted Storm's neck.

"How did you find your way to the second entrance?" he asked Elenna.

Elenna held up the amulet. "You said we could aways trust this," his friend replied.

Silver sniffed at the scales in Tom's hand, and then whined.

"Let's hope these scales can help us," Tom said, slipping them into the leather bag that held the rest of Freya's prizes. He shuddered as he heard a final roar from the bear.

"Velmal's creatures are everywhere," he said, as they turned back towards the icy plains. "And we're only halfway through our Quest."

Who knew what lay ahead?

CHAPTER FIVE

A BEAST IN CHAINS

Dusk was falling as the amulet led them across open snowfields. Finally, they came to a road rutted by frozen cartwheel tracks.

"We're getting close to a village," Elenna said.

Tom's eyes were drawn to a light on the horizon. At first he thought it was the glow of the setting sun, but then he spotted a smudge of flames and smoke.

"Something's on fire," he said to Elenna. "They might need help."

Tom dug his heels into Storm's side, and the stallion galloped along the road. His hooves squelched in the snow, and it splattered up Tom's legs. Soon they came upon fences and small huts.

Tom slowed when he saw a group of four travellers, wrapped in furs. They were laughing and patting each other on the back. As Tom and Elenna passed, they looked up.

"That's a fine horse," said one young man. "Have you come to see the ice man?"

The ice man? Tom felt a prickle of anxiety. It couldn't be Koldo, could it? Surely, the people of Gwildor wouldn't be smiling as they spoke about a Beast. Not if Velmal had enchanted it.

"What do you know of the ice man?" asked Elenna.

"Why, that he's made of ice, of course," laughed the man. "And that people are coming to Freeshor from all over Gwildor to see him."

"Freeshor?" said Tom.

The man looked at them, frowning. "You really are lost, aren't you! Never mind though, the ice man's not going anywhere. You should go and see him."

Tom spurred Storm on again, and they left the group behind.

In the narrow streets of Freeshor, children were playing, wrapped up against the cold. Smoke came from the chimneys and cooking aromas wafted out of an open window. Tom was glad to be back in a town. There didn't seem to be any sign of a fire and nobody was panicking.

"Everything seems at peace," said Elenna. "I don't understand."

Tom shook his head. "Me neither. It seems these people are living within a stone's throw of the Beast, yet they don't seem to fear it at all." The amulet couldn't be wrong, could it?

Soon they reached the market square, with stalls selling bolts of thick cloth, and roasted chestnuts. Sled-marks crisscrossed the packed snow, and a group of tethered dogs growled uneasily at Silver.

As Tom and Elenna dismounted, Tom unsheathed his sword and held

it in his left hand. His right hand
was still throbbing with the pain of
Krabb's poison.

"Why do you have your sword
out?" asked Elenna, frowning.

Tom's eyes scanned the horizon.
"The people here might not be alert
to danger, but that doesn't mean the
Beast isn't ready to attack," he said.

"Hay for your horse, sir?"

Tom turned to see a boy of about
his own age. When he saw the
sword in Tom's left hand, his eyes
widened and then searched Tom's
face.

"You're him, aren't you?" said the
boy.

Tom shared an anxious look with
Elenna.

"I'm…who?" said Tom.

The boy smiled. "The son of Gwildor.

You know the prophecy:
A son of Gwildor, raised in the East,
Will come to save the kingdom's Beasts.
We've heard all about you."

Tom remembered how the fisher boy Castor had called him the Son of Gwildor, too. Then there had been the painting that he'd seen during his quest against Hawkite. It had been a picture of a boy just like Tom, but with his sword gripped in his left hand. Now, it looked as though this youngster also thought that Tom was the Son of Gwildor – whoever that was.

The boy puffed out his chest. "But you're too late. We've got it all in hand here. The ice man's imprisoned."

"Imprisoned?" said Tom. "How?"

"I'll show you," said the boy. "I'm Linus, by the way."

Linus led them through the centre of the village and along a track through a pine wood. He spoke breathlessly over his shoulder as he went.

"Freeshor's never been very popular. After all, who'd want to visit a place where it's always cold? But now we've got the ice man, all that's changed. People are coming from all over Gwildor to see our prize. Brings in good money, too..."

They passed a queue of people gathered along the path, buying snacks from the sellers who worked the crowd. Tom sheathed his sword; he didn't want to scare the villagers. He could hear the crackle of fire ahead and saw a glow between the trees. But nothing could prepare him for what he saw when he descended into the clearing.

Four huge torches, billowing smoke
and each the size of a man, were
positioned in a square on a frozen
lake. In the middle, sitting on the
ground, was…

"Koldo!" gasped Elenna.

The Beast's icy body glistened in
the firelight. Melting water streamed
over his frozen limbs. There were

four ropes around Koldo's neck, and
each was tied to one of four massive
boulders positioned between the
torches. The Beast's head sagged
between his shoulders.

Beyond the torches, men and
women waved sticks and jeered.
Others simply looked at him in
amazement.

"Well, what do you think?" said Linus proudly.

Tom was dumb with shock. Normally when he met a new Beast for the first time, the emotion that filled him was fear. But all he could feel now was pity.

"Of course," Linus continued, "we can't put the torches too close or he'd melt away to nothing. We've found this works best. He's shrunk a bit since we captured him, but he seems to be able to produce new ice all the time..."

Tom turned to Elenna and saw tears in her eyes. "It's horrible, Tom!" she said.

Looking at the Beast, Tom searched for a sign of Velmal's enchantment. All the other Beasts he'd faced in Gwildor had had something – green pincers or green feathers – but there was nothing on Koldo's body that looked bewitched. The Beast wasn't thrashing around, or trying to flee. He crouched with his head bowed.

Tom seized Linus by the arm. "I must speak with the village elders," he said.

Linus looked alarmed. "Why? Don't you want to see the ice man up close?"

"Please," said Tom. "It's important."

Linus nodded slowly and led them down another track. As the sound of the crowd died away, Tom whispered to Elenna, "I think they've made a terrible mistake…"

CHAPTER SIX

AN OLD ENEMY

They hadn't gone far when a woman's
voice rang out.

"Li-nus? Li-nus?"

"It's my mother," said their guide. "I
should have been home a while ago."

A plump woman in an apron
appeared ahead of them.

"Linus!" she said. "There you are.
Get home this instant, your dinner is
colder than the ice man."

She took Linus' arm and led him away. He called back as he went. "Down the hill, and take the left fork to the Meeting House. You'll find the Elders there."

Tom and Elenna followed his directions. Storm shivered and Silver's paws made soundless prints in the snow.

At the edge of the market square, they came across a group of locals gathered around a camp-fire, roasting a pig. A heated discussion was taking place. A tall, thin man stuffed some bread with a chunk of meat into Tom and Elenna's hands.

"Thank you," said Tom, as Elenna dropped pieces of the meat into Silver's open mouth.

"It's a pleasure," said the man. "So, what do you think?"

"About what?" Tom replied, sinking his teeth into the bread.

"About the ice man, of course! Gertrude here doesn't think we should keep him tied up, but we've never had it so good. There's meat enough for everyone now that Freeshor's such an attraction."

"Meat isn't everything," said a woman seated opposite, who Tom guessed must be Gertrude. "What about the fishing-holes, Simon? Since we've got his Royal Icy-ness there's no more fish in 'em. It's all well and good attracting people to our town, but not if they eat all our food. We've got enough meat now, but what happens when the hunting dries up?"

Tom looked at Elenna, She'd barely touched her food, and her face was furrowed with concern.

The townspeople had been kind to share their food; why couldn't Tom's friend eat?

"This shouldn't be happening to a Beast," she commented quietly to Tom. In all their Quests, they'd never seen one of their foes robbed of his dignity like this.

"You're right," he said. "Come on. Let's find the Meeting Hall."

They left the fireside and followed the path as Linus had advised. It was paved with small, flat stones. Soon, a large building came into view, looming above the path, pale blue in the moonlight. They hurried towards it and Tom placed his hands against one of the huge blocks that made up its walls.

"It's an ice castle!" he said.

A light murmur of voices came

from within the building.

"This must be the Meeting House," said Elenna. She turned to Storm and Silver and made a circular motion with her hand. Storm and Silver immediately began to amble in a circle, moving to stay warm in the chilly air.

Tom rapped his knuckles three times on the large wooden door.

"Enter!" boomed a voice.

Tom pushed open the door and stepped inside. What he saw took his breath away.

Eight tiers of steep wooden benches, covered in cushions, faced each other over a wide aisle. At least one hundred people sat on each side, all old men dressed in scarlet robes. But they weren't talking to one another, or even whispering. They were looking at an object that sat on an ice altar in the centre of the aisle. It was a shield, pulsing with a green light. Tom immediately recognised Velmal's colour of enchantment.

The shield must belong to Koldo, he thought.

It was clear that the Beast had been trapped and robbed of his shield, torn free of the evil spell of Velmal. That explained why he wasn't putting up a fight. Koldo was locked inside his fiery prison because only the fury of Velmal would make him try to break free.

A robed elder stood and faced Tom.

"I am Dylar, chief of this village. What can we do for you, stranger?"

Every face was looking at Tom and Elenna. Few of them were friendly.

"You must free the ice man," Tom said.

Laughter erupted through the ranks of elders.

"Free him?" said another elder. "Why would we? He was a curse on Freeshor."

"I know this makes no sense to

you," Tom said. "But without his shield, the ice man is no threat. You would be showing him a great kindness if you set him free."

"He talks nonsense," a voice cried out. "The Beast is our saviour, our wealth."

"He is innocent!" shouted Elenna. "If you keep him trapped he'll die—"

More shouting drowned out her voice, until Dylar raised his hands for quiet. He stepped down from his seat and walked towards Tom.

"We don't often welcome strangers into our councils, boy." He was calm, but firm. "I suggest you leave us to—"

A shadow detached itself from the wall and flashed across the room. The village chief was suddenly thrown to the floor.

A cloaked figure, tall and lean, stood before Tom. A slender hand went up to the hood and slowly drew it back. Tom recognised the thin face and the long hair, black and slick.

"Freya!" he gasped.

Gwildor's Mistress of the Beasts stared back with glinting dark eyes.

"Of course. Who else?" she hissed.

CHAPTER SEVEN

THE SHIELD OF VELMAL

Dylar regained his senses and struggled to his feet. "Seize her!" he yelled.

Freya aimed a kick that sent the old man sprawling on the floor again. Tom and Elenna dashed to his side.

The elders clambered off their seats and rushed towards Freya. She easily swatted aside the first man who appoached her. Another came towards her, but she picked him up and threw him across the room at a group of advancing men.

"Are you all right?" Tom asked Dylar, helping him up. The chief's face was pale.

"Who is that woman?" he gasped.

Freya was pushing her way through the crowd, scattering the elders with her fists and feet. Her savage movements were a blur, but the sound of her blows left Tom in no doubt that she was a warrior to be reckoned with. If she had been fighting for good, Tom would have admired her, but why was she using her powers to harm innocent people?

"What does she want?" asked Dylar. The answer was obvious to Tom. Freya was beating a path towards the room's centre.

"She wants the shield," he said.

Elenna had lined up an arrow and was tracking Freya's progress across the Meeting Hall.

"I can't risk a shot, Tom," she said. "I might hit one of the elders."

Cries of pain went up around the hall, as more of the Freeshor Councillors fell before Freya. The Mistress of the Beasts had reached the shield. She leapt up onto the ice altar.

"This belongs to my master!" she shouted, and snatched up the shield. Her face, bathed in green light, twisted with cruel joy.

Elenna loosed an arrow, which sailed over the heads of the elders. But Freya dodged to one side and watched it flash past.

"It will take more than your knitting needles to stop me!" she bellowed. She looped a strap over her head, so that the shield hung from her back, and leapt across the seats. Tom left Dylar's side and headed towards her, heaving himself through the crowd of fleeing people. Freya climbed the tiers, quick as a rat, until she reached the top. She was still a long way from the hall's only exit.

"There's nowhere to run!" Tom

shouted, drawing his sword with his left hand. "Give yourself up!"

Freya sneered, then lifted the shield above her head. She smashed its rim hard into the wall. A great crack opened up with an ear-splitting roar. Tom plunged after her, but the crowd was too dense. She hammered the wall again, and one of the giant ice-blocks fell away. With a yell of triumph she slipped through the gap and dashed out into the night. Tom looked back and yelled to Elenna: "We need to go after Freya!"

Elenna nodded and made her way towards the door. Tom climbed through the hole and perched on the ledge. He was at least twenty paces above the ground, but he could see Freya sneaking between two wooden buildings beside the Meeting Hall.

How had she got down so quickly? But, knowing he had Arcta's golden feather to protect him he jumped off the ledge and landed softly on the ground below, holding his shield above his head. Elenna emerged at the front of the building.

"Did you see where she went?" his friend shouted. Silver was at her side, and Storm stamped his hooves.

Tom pointed. "This way."

They dived into the alley and soon emerged into the pine trees that grew along the slope. Tom had a hunch where Freya was heading: to Koldo. Shouts and screams echoed around the village as news spread of the commotion in the Hall. Tom caught sight of Freya, darting between the trees. The green glow of the shield flitted in and out of sight. Tom saw

two men jump into her path, but
Freya charged straight at them and
knocked them aside with the green
shield. Could anything stop her?

The yellow glow cast by the torches
imprisoning Koldo lay ahead. Tom
slid down a snowy embankment. He
was sure Elenna wasn't far behind,
but he daren't stop; he couldn't risk
losing Freya. He heaved his body
through a snowdrift and over a small
ditch, then saw his foe ahead. Freya
had stopped and was facing him. Tom
was pleased to see that she was
breathless from her flight.

So you're not invincible, after all! he
thought.

Koldo sat dejected on the ice, the
torches blazing around him. He
looked even smaller than when Tom
had last seen him, and was now

barely bigger than a normal man. So
much for the magnificent Ice Beast of
Gwildor! The spectators backed away
when Freya approached.

"Don't come any closer," Freya
warned Tom, "or your death will
be certain."

Tom drew his sword and held it aloft. "I'm not afraid of death. Or you."

He took a step forwards, but felt unsure of himself. Could he fight Freya with his injured right hand?

The wicked Mistress of the Beasts slammed the green shield against the ground and Tom felt the lake's frozen surface shake beneath him. Several cracks snaked out across the ice. So, that was Freya's plan! She struck again, and the cracks widened. Tom felt the frozen surface beneath his feet tilt dangerously, and he almost fell. "Tom," shouted Elenna. "Be careful! You'll fall through the ice."

While Tom tried to steady himself on the shifting lake, Freya turned to Koldo. She placed the shield face down on the ground then kicked it towards the Beast. It shot across the ice until it was a few paces away from him, within the fiery cordon. There was nothing Tom could do.

Everyone was silent as Koldo stared at the shield glowing beside him. There was only the creaking of the ice.

"Pick it up!" bellowed Freya. Koldo looked at her. If he understood the words, he didn't move. Then he stared at the shield again. Were those tears in his eyes, or melting ice?

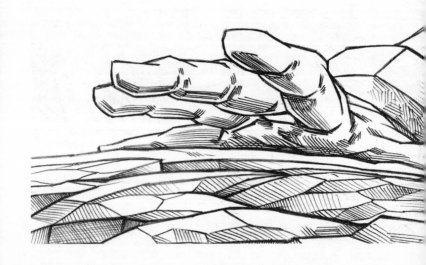

He's afraid, Tom realised. *He wants to be good!*

"Take it!" hissed Freya.

Don't do it, Tom begged silently.

Slowly, Koldo's hand reached out and gripped the shield.

CHAPTER EIGHT

TACKLING THE ICE GIANT

As soon as Koldo touched the shield, he grew larger and stronger.

"My work is done!" laughed Freya. She turned and sprinted away, bounding across the still, frozen banks of the lake.

Koldo stood up, looming as tall as two men. The ropes around his neck tightened and then snapped. People yelled with fear and began to panic.

"The fire will hold him!" cried a woman.

But she was wrong. Koldo swung a foot and kicked one of the torches from the ground. It arced into the night sky like a shooting star. In the space of a few heartbeats, Koldo had turned from a pathetic captive into a terrible monster. He was Velmal's once again. From the frozen lake's shore, Tom's stallion whinnied.

"Keep Storm away from the middle," shouted Tom to Elenna. 'The ice isn't thick enough to take him."

Tom sheathed his sword and began to pick his way across the ice, but he barely took a step before a frozen fragment tipped dangerously and he was sliding towards a broken edge. He dug his heels in and just managed to stop his body from plunging into the freezing water below.

Koldo had no such problem. With each massive stride new ice formed beneath his feet like the roots of a tree. He was in no danger of falling through. The Beast towered over the people of Freeshor, growing larger with every step. With one sweep of his arm, three people were scattered across the ice like skittles. Silver bravely darted between Koldo's legs, and for a moment the Ice Giant was distracted. The Beast swatted at Silver, but the wolf was too quick. Some villagers scrambled to safety, but Tom needed to come up with a plan before someone was killed.

He struggled to his feet and held his arms out to balance himself as the broken ice rocked dangerously.

How could he fight like this? There must be something he could do, something to help him stay upright...

Of course...the scales!

He looked back at Elenna, standing with Silver and Storm near the shore where the ice was thick. She looked on, her bow at the ready. Against Koldo, arrows would be useless. Carefully, Tom shuffled towards her, keeping his gaze firmly on Koldo. Finally back beside Storm, he fished into the saddle-bag with freezing fingers and pulled out the leather sack. Inside was the set of scales.

"I hope I'm right about this," he muttered to himself.

"What are you doing?" asked his friend. "We can't run away."

"I'm not," said Tom. "Wait and see..."

He heard Koldo roar. The trapped

villagers were making a bid to escape, darting under Koldo's legs as he tried to snatch at them. But the ice cracked beneath them and they toppled into the freezing water. Koldo tipped back his head and the mocking sound that emerged from his mouth was the unmistakable laughter of Velmal.

"Help the villagers," Tom said. "I'm going after Koldo."

"Good luck," his friend replied, moving carefully around the edge of the thicker ice.

Tom stepped back onto the floating ice, holding the scales. It was time to test his theory. As soon as he felt unsteady and his feet began to slide, the scales tipped in the opposite direction and he regained his balance. He took another small step and the ice rocked again; and again the scales righted him.

At least now I understand how this prize helps, Tom thought.

Koldo turned to see his approach, and stamped on the ice. A web of thin cracks spread out towards Tom's feet, but he stayed upright. To one side, he saw Silver plunge his snout into the icy water and heave out a bedraggled, shivering villager. Elenna was directing others across thicker patches of ice to safe ground.

When he decided he was close enough to the Beast, Tom shoved the scales inside his fur coat and rushed forwards, reaching out for the shield. His fingers brushed the rim, but Koldo whipped it away and Tom sprawled across the ice. His injured hand was caught beneath him and he couldn't help but cry out.

He leapt up as he saw a flash of green to his left. He ducked as the green shield sliced the air above his head. He had no doubt the blow would have crushed his skull.

The ground rumbled as Koldo shifted position, then kicked out.

Tom spun and dodged the giant foot.
He lifted his own shield.

"While there's blood in my veins,"
Tom cried out, "this fight *will* end!"
Then he brought the shield down as
hard as he could onto the Beast's foot,
smashing huge chips of ice away.

Koldo didn't even make a sound.

Tom stared, horrified, as the ice

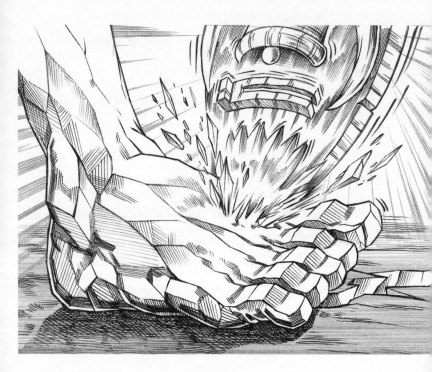

reformed over the Beast's foot, leaving no trace of the wound. He looked up and saw the Beast's head turned towards his own. A cold smile opened like a crack in the Ice Giant's face. The Beast lashed out a sudden, violent kick and Tom was lifted into the air. He slammed back onto the ice, skidding against a snow drift. Chilled water soaked into his tunic as he tried to get his breath. Koldo strode towards him.

Move! Tom commanded himself. But his limbs were too slow to respond and his head felt fuzzy. The Beast split into two as Tom's vision blurred.

Koldo lifted a foot again, high above Tom.

Elenna's voice sounded far off: "No!"

Then the icy foot stamped down.

CHAPTER NINE

THE FINAL BATTLE

Tom half slid, half rolled away and heard a mighty crunch. Koldo's foot plunged through the patch of ice where Tom had been lying. As the Ice Beast struggled to free himself, he let out a roar of fury. Tom climbed to his feet. The cold was draining his strength.

It was hopeless. How could he face a Beast who couldn't be defeated?

He had to get that green shield. That was the only hope. Koldo lunged at him. Tom stumbled backwards towards the thin ice. He could not pull out the scales because he needed both hands for his sword and shield. Beneath the ice he could see water, dark and deadly. If he fell in, he would drown before anyone could reach him.

Koldo strode towards him. Each step was sure-footed because the ice instantly thickened where his feet fell. Tom backed away, slipping with every step, hoping only that the Beast would strike with his green shield – anything to give Tom a chance to snatch it.

But the Beast wasn't foolish. Tom could see he was biding his time, driving Tom further onto the thin ice at the centre of the frozen lake.

Tom would have to gamble if he was to win this battle.

He waited until Koldo was close, then pretended to stumble. The Beast swiped with his left arm. Tom easily ducked, then hooked his own arms around the Beast's wrist. He clung on and was lifted off the ice.

Koldo raged, shaking his arm violently from side to side, but Tom held on. Every jerk sent a lightning bolt of pain through his right hand. The ice was so cold that his fingers stuck to it, burning his skin. Then Koldo brought his other arm across and batted Tom away. The skin on his hands tore as he was sent cartwheeling through the air. The scales fell from his coat and clattered away across the icy ground. Tom hit the ice and slid along, until freezing water enveloped his arm. He was at the ice-rim, with the water lapping at his side. Any further and he would have drowned.

The scales! Tom thought. He looked around, but couldn't see them anywhere.

Koldo was walking towards him,

larger and stronger than ever.

Across the ice, Elenna was mounted on Storm, holding a flaming torch in each hand.

"Tom," she shouted. "Use one of these."

It might work, Tom thought, but she was too far away. And could he even catch it with his left hand?

Elenna threw a torch and it spun, trailing flames. Tom reached up with his left hand, but the torch sailed past his fingers and skidded across the ice.

Koldo moved between him and Elenna. His hand reached down and gripped Tom around the waist. The icy fingers tightened and Tom could hardly breath. Koldo's eyes, black holes in the ice, stared through him.

The hand crushed against his ribs until he was sure his bones would break, but he gritted his teeth.

I won't give Koldo the satisfaction of crying out, Tom promised himself.

Suddenly, a shower of sparks fell over them and Koldo's head snapped around with a jerk. A flaming torch dropped through the air and plunged into the water with a sizzle. Elenna had thrown the second torch at Koldo's head! The Beast was stunned and his grip around Tom's middle weakened.

Tom reached for his sword with his right hand and swung it in an arc. It thudded into Koldo's left shoulder, and cleaved into the ice, sending up a shower of icy shards. Koldo bellowed in pain. Tom tugged the sword loose and swung again. The blade buried deeper into the joint, but still not all the way through.

Koldo uttered an eerie groan as
Tom swung the blade for the third
time, slicing through the arm
completely. It dropped to the ground,
together with the shield. The frozen
limb shattered into a thousand pieces,
and the thin ice cracked. For a
moment the shield seemed to float

on the surface, but then the dark
water swallowed it up. Tom watched
as the green glow sank into the
depths.

Relief swept over him: Koldo
was free!

The Beast's cry of pain filled Tom's ears, and the hand released him.

Tom plummeted through the air until his feet hit the frozen lake. The ice cracked and he plunged into the water. Cold enveloped his body, and his heart seemed to stop. Freezing water invaded his mouth, his nostrils, his ears.

He tried to thrash up to the surface, but his strength was being sapped away. His mind whirled with confusion.

One thought was clear: he'd never see the light of day again.

CHAPTER TEN

THE DEPTHS OF EVIL

The cold gripped Tom like a fist. His lungs were ready to burst.

A white shape glowed in the watery shadows, getting bigger. Tom felt himself drawn towards it. He was moving quickly through the water now, his lungs screaming with pain. Unable to hold his breath any longer, he sucked in.

But it wasn't water that filled his lungs. It was air!

Tom spluttered and rubbed the water from his eyes. He was looking down on the frozen lake. Freezing water was pouring off his clothes. He struggled to turn over and found himself staring into a face he knew well: Koldo. Tom was sitting on his huge, icy palm. Koldo had reached into the lake and rescued him.

Joy surged through his shivering limbs. Koldo was good again – for ever, this time. Another Beast of Gwildor was free!

The Ice Giant crossed the icy lake in mighty steps and gently placed Tom on the ground. Elenna rushed over.

"Oh, Tom. I thought you were dead. I thought…"

"I…I…I'm fine," he said, his teeth chattering.

"Here," said his friend, placing her own furs around him. "You're almost blue!"

"My…my shield," Tom said. "Nanook's bell."

Elenna brought Tom's shield close and, as he rubbed the bell, he began to feel warmer.

"I have to thank you," said Tom. "If you hadn't thrown that torch, Koldo would have crushed me."

Elenna smiled. "His crushing days are over now. Velmal's curse is gone."

"And the green shield is lost for ever," said Tom.

Beside them, Koldo made a noise like laughter.

"Look, Tom!" said Elenna. "His arm!"

Tom gazed at their new friend in amazement. The severed arm was already growing back. Koldo leaned down and packed some snow against the new limb to make it bigger.

Tom patted Storm and the stallion nudged his nose against Tom's shoulder.

The good Beast crouched down beside Tom, then reached out. Tom saw that the Ice Giant was holding something in his hand, an offering.

"The scales!" Elenna exclaimed. "You dropped them when you fell."

Tom took them, and placed them in his saddle bag, along with the other magical prizes.

"Thank you," he said.

The Beast straightened up, then nodded. He turned and walked back towards the village.

"Do you think he'll be safe there?" Elenna asked.

"The villagers have seen enough to understand what caused Koldo's violence. Only an evil enchantment would make a Beast behave like that. My guess is they'll learn to live alongside one another now."

From the sky, a beam of purple light struck the ice and grew into a disc. The earth shook and Silver growled. In the middle of the disc, the outline of a figure appeared.

"Velmal," Tom muttered.

"Of course," replied a voice with an angry snarl. "What did you think? That by freeing one of the Beasts you would defeat me?"

"Leave us alone!" shouted Elenna. "We're not afraid."

Velmal snorted. "Well, you should

be. You think you can save the people of Gwildor, but you're mistaken. I make you a solemn oath that the next Quest will be your last. None of you will leave Gwildor alive."

Tom drew his sword, but Velmal vanished in a plume of purple smoke. Tom didn't know if the evil wizard could hear him, but he shouted across the ice anyway. "While there's blood in my veins, no Beast will be a prisoner of yours!"

Tom and Elenna gathered their possessions and led Storm and Silver away from the village of Freeshor. It was too close to dawn to make camp now, and there were two more Beasts still under Velmal's spells to save before Tom could go home and see his father, Taladon, again. But with Elenna, Storm and Silver beside him, Tom knew he would succeed.

Here's a sneak preview of Tom's
next exciting adventure!

Meet

TREMA
THE EARTH LORD

Only Tom can free the Beasts from
Velmal's wicked enchantment...

PROLOGUE

The full moon shed a cold light over the plains of Gwildor. A chill wind bent the grass and rustled the leaves.

The moonlight picked out the dark figure of a man, scuttling from one patch of shadow to the next. His hair and beard were ragged; he wore rough woollen trousers and a jerkin fastened at the waist with a rope. A spade was tucked into the rope. He glanced furtively over his shoulder, as if he was afraid he would be followed.

At last the man halted in a spot where a few sharp stones poked through the grass. "This'll do," he muttered, with another swift look around. He let out a hoarse chuckle.

"You're a fine fellow, Ally," he mumbled to himself. "And soon you'll be rich!"

Ally pulled out the spade and began to dig, slowly at first, then faster as sweat plastered his hair to his forehead and spread dark stains on his tunic. He threw the earth aside as he dug deeper into the ground.

As Ally bent over the spade, his jerkin gaped

open and a soft leather roll fell to the ground. Muttering a curse, Ally threw the spade aside and grabbed the roll. He started to thrust it inside his jerkin again, then paused.

"My treasure will look even more beautiful by the light of the moon," he murmured.

Smiling to himself, Ally unfurled the leather roll to reveal a set of tiny silver skulls strung on a chain. He held it up to see it glitter in the moonlight.

"You're mine now. I'm sure your owner will never miss you!" he said, laughing.

Ally's smile faded as a cold wind whistled around him, and he cast a nervous glance all around. He could see nothing but the empty plain, and a few cattle grazing in the distance. But he still couldn't push away the feeling that he was being watched.

"I won't take any chances," he promised himself. "I'll bury my treasure here until it's safe to come back and collect it."

Carefully he put the stolen silver skulls back inside the leather roll and set it down beside the hole. Then he dug with his spade again, leaning further and further into the hiding place he was making.

Suddenly, the ground beneath Ally's spade seemed to shift. Long cracks zig-zagged out from the hole. Ally felt the earth shift underneath his feet; soil erupted into the air. He let out a cry of terror as he was thrown to the ground.

**Follow this Quest to the end in
TREMA THE EARTH LORD.**

Win an exclusive
Beast Quest T-shirt and goody bag!

In every Beast Quest book the Beast Quest logo is hidden in one of the pictures. Find the logos in books 25 to 30 and make a note of which pages they appear on. Write the six page numbers on a postcard and send it in to us. Each month we will draw one winner to receive a Beast Quest T-shirt and goody bag.

THE BEAST QUEST COMPETITION:
THE SHADE OF DEATH

Orchard Books
338 Euston Road, London NW1 3BH

Australian readers should email:
childrens.books@hachette.com.au

New Zealand readers should write to:
Beast Quest Competition
4 Whetu Place, Mairangi Bay, Auckland, NZ
or email: childrensbooks@hachette.co.nz

Only one entry per child.
Final draw: 29 October 2010

You can also enter this competition
via the Beast Quest website: www.beastquest.co.uk

Join the Quest,
Join the Tribe

www.beastquest.co.uk

Have you checked out the all-new Beast Quest website?
It's the place to go for games, downloads, activities,
sneak previews and lots of fun!

You can read all about your favourite Beasts, download
free screensavers and desktop wallpapers for your
computer, and even challenge your friends
to a Beast Tournament.

Sign up to the newsletter at www.beastquest.co.uk
to receive exclusive extra content and the opportunity
to enter special members-only competitions. We'll send
you up-to-date info on all the Beast Quest books,
including the next exciting series which features
six brand-new Beasts!

Beast Quest®

Series 5
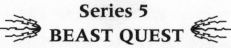
BEAST QUEST

Tom must travel to Gwildor, Avantia's twin kingdom, to free six new Beasts from an evil enchantment...

978 1 40830 437 2

978 1 40830 438 9

978 1 40830 439 6

978 1 40830 440 2

978 1 40830 441 9

978 1 40830 442 6

978 1 40830 436 5

Can Tom rescue the precious Cup of Life from a deadly two-headed demon?

Series 6: WORLD OF CHAOS
COMING SOON!

KOMODO

978 1 40830 723 6

MURO
THE EYE MONSTER

978 1 40830 724 3

FANG

978 1 40830 725 0

MURK

978 1 40830 726 7

TERRA
CURSE OF THE FOREST

978 1 40830 727 4

VESPICK

978 1 40830 728 1

CRETA

978 1 40830 735 9

SPECIAL BUMPER EDITION!

Does Tom have the strength to triumph over cunning Creta?

KOLDO
THE ARCTIC WARRIOR

In Gwildor's arctic region is deadly Koldo, the Arctic Warrior, who uses his ferocious club and fists to batter his enemies.

Age	335
Power	183
Magic Level	166
Fright Factor	84

Beast Quest is a registered trademark of Working Partners Limited

MAGIC SCALES

Whenever Tom feels unsteady on his feet these magical scales tip in the opposite direction and help him to regain his balance.

Age	264
Power	223
Magic Level	172
Fright Factor	68

Beast Quest is a registered trademark of Working Partners Limited

NANOOK
THE SNOW MONSTER

Nanook the snow monster protects the icy plains in the north of Avantia. One blow from her paw can crack a lake of solid ice!

Age	335
Power	165
Magic Level	131
Fright Factor	73

Beast Quest is a registered trademark of Working Partners Limited

ENCHANTED BELL

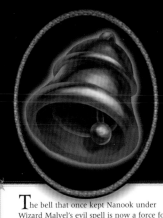

The bell that once kept Nanook under Wizard Malvel's evil spell is now a force for good. Placed in Tom's shield, it protects him against extreme cold.

Age	96
Power	80
Magic Level	125
Fright Factor	9

Beast Quest is a registered trademark of Working Partners Limited

Fight the Beasts,
Fear the Magic

www.beastquest.co.uk
ORCHARD BOOKS

Fight the Beasts,
Fear the Magic

www.beastquest.co.uk
ORCHARD BOOKS

Fight the Beasts,
Fear the Magic

www.beastquest.co.uk
ORCHARD BOOKS

Fight the Beasts,
Fear the Magic

www.beastquest.co.uk
ORCHARD BOOKS